text by JILL BARBER
art by SYDNEY SMITH

NIMBUS
PUBLISHING

Nimbus Publishing Limited
3731 Mackintosh St, Halifax, NS B3K 5A5
(902) 455-4286 nimbus.ca

Printed and bound in China
NB1102

Cover and interior design: Heather Bryan
Author photo: Candace Meyer
Illustrator photo: D. Edwards

Library and Archives Canada Cataloguing in Publication

Barber, Jill, 1980-, author
Music is for everyone / text by Jill Barber; art by Sydney Smith.

Issued in print and electronic formats.
ISBN 978-1-77108-150-4 (bound).—ISBN 978-1-77108-151-1 (pdf)

1. Music—Juvenile literature. I. Smith, Sydney, 1980-, illustrator
II. Title.

ML3928.B234 2014   j780   C2013-908092-9
                                         C2013-908093-7

Nimbus Publishing acknowledges the financial support for its publishing activities from the Government of Canada through the Canada Book Fund (CBF) and the Canada Council for the Arts, and from the Province of Nova Scotia through Film & Creative Industries Nova Scotia. We are pleased to work in partnership with Film & Creative Industries Nova Scotia to develop and promote our creative industries for the benefit of all Nova Scotians.

For Joshua, may there always
be a song in your heart.
- J.B.

For Zoe.
- S.S.

MUSIC is
For EVERYONE

There are so many ways
To join in the fun

We can clap our hands
Or stomp our feet

We can sing out loud
Or move to the beat

We can play classical
in a symphony
With a big trombone
Or a tympani

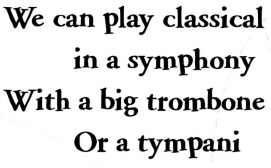

We can sing a lullaby
As soft as a petal

Or shout out loud
Like it's heavy metal

We can bring out the sun
On a rainy day
With some mellow beats
and a little reggae

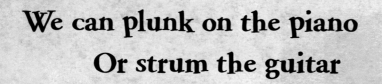

We can plunk on the piano
Or strum the guitar

We can pretend we're up on stage
Like a big pop star

We can sing old standards
Like a real jazz cat

We can make up silly words
They call that scat

We can play the drums
    We can make a racket
But if you're in a marching band
    Don't forget your jacket!

Or have a mighty
fine time
Playing old
Bebop

We can chant special prayers
Around a big campfire

or sing sweet harmonies
As part of a choir

We can pick up the banjo
       With an old country twang

Or move to the groove
Aboard the soul music train

We can tell a good story
In a sweet folk song
Teach everyone the chorus
and have a big singalong

We can sing
an operetta
With a big
booming voice

or hum a quiet little tune
It's your choice!

It's fun to explore
        Every kind of way
That we make music
        together...

...So let's sing
and play!